By Jerry Lott

Pictures by BRAINYINK

Meowy Christmas
Published by BigStar Publishing

Designs and pictures were taken from freepik.com/Designed by brgfx under freemium license, vecteezy.com under freemium license, Creativefabrica.com under premium license, and Canva.com under premium license and some where generated by Artificial Intelligence with extensive editing

This Book
is dedicated
To all
Awesome
Kids

Christmas cheers to the

BEARY best bear

HOPPY holidays to the
sweetest bunny out there

Christmas HEDGEHUGS

to you my precious one

May you **BEE** Merry forever my very beloved hun

Happy Christmas to you my

PAW-SOME sweetie pie

Merry everything TWEET-
heart - perched on trees or
high in the sky

Christmas hugs and warm
FISHES to the bestest fish

May your Christmas,
my DEER , be adorned
with cheers, that's all
I wish

FURRY Christmas
SQUEAK-heart, may you
find joy and cheers

MEOWY cuddly Christmas sweetie - now and all the years

And You My Dear Merry Christmas

www.ingramcontent.com/pod-product-compliance
Lightning Source LLC
Chambersburg PA
CBHW042109160726
48295CB00017B/1041

* 9 7 8 1 7 6 3 6 5 8 5 5 4 *